For my boy, Mills,
with all my love.

Copyright © 2023 by Dawn Masi

All rights reserved. Published in the United States by Doubleday, an imprint of Random House
Children's Books, a division of Penguin Random House LLC, New York.

Doubleday is a registered trademark and the Doubleday colophon is a trademark of
Penguin Random House LLC.

Visit us on the Web! rhcbooks.com

Educators and librarians, for a variety of teaching tools, visit us at RHTeachersLibrarians.com

*Library of Congress Cataloging-in-Publication Data*

Name: Masi, Dawn, author, illustrator.

Title: B my name is boy : a song of celebration from Australia to Zimbabwe /
written and illustrated by Dawn Masi.

Description: First edition. | New York : Doubleday, 2023. | Audience: Ages 3–7.

Summary: "An alphabetical celebration of boys around the world, with countries, names,
and character traits from A to Z" —Provided by publisher.

Identifiers: LCCN 2022021376 (print) | LCCN 2022021377 (ebook) |
ISBN 978-0-593-48712-9 (hardcover) | ISBN 978-0-593-48713-6 (library binding) |
ISBN 978-0-593-48714-3 (ebook)

Subjects: CYAC: Boys—Fiction. | Individuality—Fiction. | Alphabet. | LCGFT: Picture books.

Classification: LCC PZ7.1.M3755 Bam 2021 (print) | LCC PZ7.1.M3755 (ebook) | DDC [E]—dc23

MANUFACTURED IN CHINA

10 9 8 7 6 5 4 3 2 1

First Edition

# B MY NAME IS BOY

Written and illustrated by

## DAWN MASI

Doubleday Books
for Young Readers

Throughout the land, across the sea, let's find friends from **A** to **Z**.
Come join in—one, two, three! Bounce a ball and play with me. . . .

EARTH DAY
EVERY DAY!

A, my name is **ARCHIE**, and my brother's name is **ARLO**.
We come from **AUSTRALIA**, and we can **ADVOCATE**.

ONE EARTH
ONE CHANCE

**B**, my name is **BRUNO**, and my best friend's name is **BENICIO**.
We come from **BRAZIL**, and we can **BUILD**.

C, my name is **COOPER**, and my cousin's name is **CALEB**.
We come from **CANADA**, and we can **CAMP**.

**D**, my name is **DANILO**, and my father's name is **DIEGO**.
We come from the **DOMINICAN REPUBLIC**, and we can **DANCE**.

**E**, my name is **EMAD**, and my neighbor's name is **EZZAT**.
We come from **EGYPT**, and we can **EMBRACE**.

**F**, my name is **FABRICE**,
and my grandad's name is **FERNAND**.
We come from **FRANCE**,
and we can **FISH**.

**G**, my name is **GUILLE**,
and my papa's name is **GABRIEL**.
We come from **GUATEMALA**,
and we can **GROW**.

**H**, my name is **HENRIK**,
and my brother's name is **HUNOR**.
We come from **HUNGARY**,
and we can **HELP**.

I, my name is **INGI**, and my classmate's name is **IVAR**.
We come from **ICELAND**, and we can **IMAGINE**.

**J**, my name is **JUNIOR**,
and my uncle's name is **JEVAUN**.
We come from **JAMAICA**,
and we can **JOURNEY**.

**K**, my name is **KAIRAT**,
and my nephew's name is **KANYSH**.
We come from **KAZAKHSTAN**,
and we can **KISS**.

L, my name is **LAURIS**, and my teacher's name is **LUDIS**.
We come from **LATVIA**, and we can **LEND**.

M, my name is **MONKHBAT**, and my cousin's name is **MENDBAYAR**.
We come from **MONGOLIA**, and we can **MEND**.

, my name is **NIRMAL**, and my neighbor's name is **NABIN**.
We come from **NEPAL**, and we can **NOURISH**.

O, my name is **OMAR**, and my uncle's name is **OBAID**.
We come from **OMAN**, and we can **OBSERVE**.

P, my name is **PABLO**, and my papa's name is **PELAGIO**.
We come from **PARAGUAY**, and we can **PAINT**.

**Q**, my name is **QABIL**, and my classmate's name is **QAMAR**.
We come from **QATAR**, and we can **QUESTION**.

R, my name is **RADU**,
and my best friend's name is **RAZVAN**.
We come from **ROMANIA**,
and we can **RECONCILE**.

S, my name is **SEYDOU**, and my father's name is **SOULEYMANE**. We come from **SENEGAL**, and we can **SOOTHE**.

T, my name is **THOBIAS**,
and my teammate's name is **TITUS**.
We come from **TANZANIA**,
and we can **TEACH**.

**U**, my name is **UPTON**, and my buddy's name is **ULYSSES**.
We come from the **USA**, and we can **UNDERSTAND**.

V, my name is **VIÉN**,
and my best friend's name is **VUONG**.
We come from **VIETNAM**,
and we can **VOLUNTEER**.

**W**, my name is **WILLIAM**, and my grandpa's name is **WYNFORD**.
We come from **WALES**, and we can **WEAVE**.

**X**, my name is **SIXTO**, and my stepdad's name is **MÁXIMO**.
We come from **MEXICO**, and we can **EXPLORE**.

Y, my name is **YASIN**, and my cousin's name is **YAZEED**.
We come from **YEMEN**, and we can **YIELD**.

**Z**, my name is **ZIVAI**, and my brother's name is **ZORORO**.
We come from **ZIMBABWE**, and we can **ZIP**.

Now it's your turn. Tell me about you.
What is your name, and what can **YOU** do?

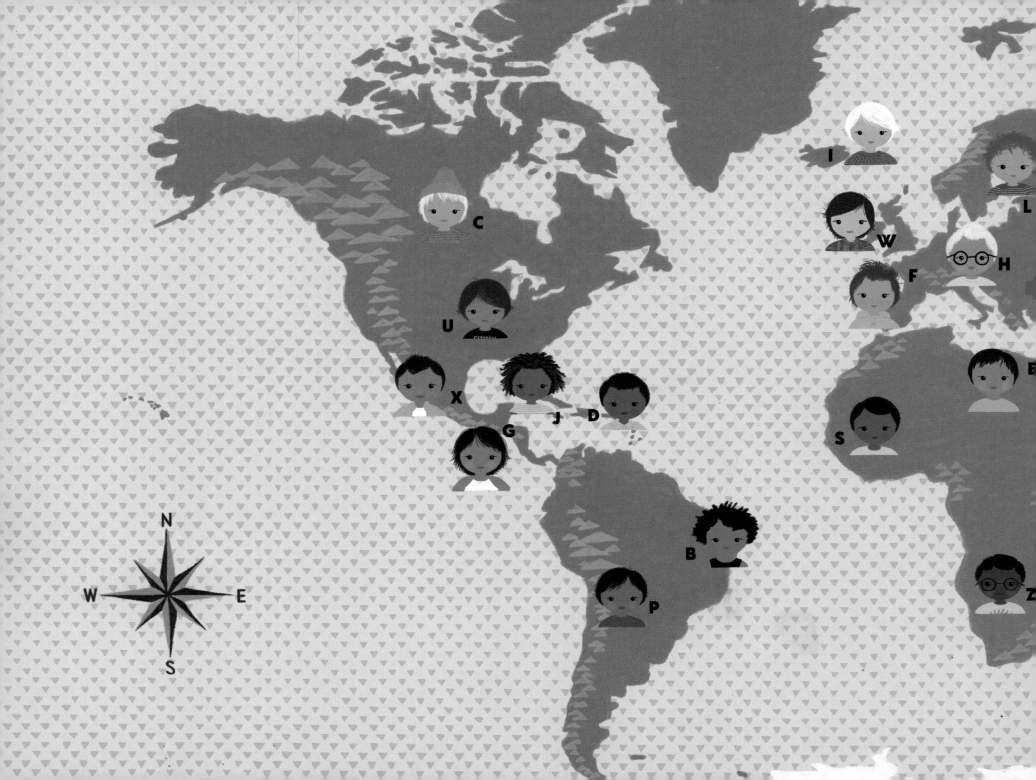